FOREST FAIRIES

by
CLARA
INGRAM
JUDSON

ILLUS-
TRATIONS
by
MAGINEL
WRIGHT
ENRIGHT

Windjammer *Publishing*

FAIRY NAMES

T HERE were so many, many fairies in the forest, and they were all so much alike, that it was hard work even for them to tell one from the other. So the Queen Fairy said, 'I'm going to give each of you a number; then when I call one of you, you can tell who I want.'

The bigger fairies helped her, and they called all through the forest, 'When the sun is high in the sky, come to the Queen's Green Palace to be numbered!'

The Queen, of course, had many palaces, as all queens do. There was a pink one east of the forest, where the sun rose, and a Crystal Palace where the brook jumped down over the rocks, and a Green Palace in the heart of the forest. To enter it, the Queen went to the greenest, quietest part of the forest, and there was a mossy cave all arched over with branches of trees

The birds would come to drink at the pool.

and shrubs covered with white blossoms and green leaves.

Right in the centre, in front of the door of the cave, was a mossy green throne where the Queen could sit. And just a little farther out was a tall, pale green flower – we call it Jack-in-the-pulpit now – and in it the Queen could sit when she wished to be high up above the other fairies, or to see a long distance.

At one side of the palace was a tiny little brook. The water in it ran very quietly and gently, making dainty little pools that the Queen used for mirrors. She liked very much to sit in her high flower throne and let the wind wave her over the water pool so she could see herself and the green leaves overhead reflected in the clear water. Sometimes she would reach out her hands, and the tiny fishes would wave their fins and flash a signal of greeting to her. The birds would come to drink at the pool and stay and talk with the Queen, and even the water spiders would weave designs for her on the surface of her pool. Of course she liked her Green Palace!

When it was nearly noon on the day the fairies were to be numbered, the Queen went to the dressing

They called in the spiders, who were dressmakers to the Queen.

room of the Green Palace to array herself in her most queenly robes. She put on soft white skirts made from the thinnest flower petals, then white silk stockings and slippers carved from a pearl shell. Her dress, which was made of white, satin water-lily petals, was put on her by her maids of honour. When all else was ready, they called in the gray spiders, who were dressmakers to the Queen, and they went up and down all over her dress until they covered it every bit with silvery cobwebs of lace.

The Queen was beautiful to look at, and all the fairy maids who helped dress her were very proud of her, for she was kind and wise as well as beautiful. When all was ready, the Queen put on her head her golden crown with the star on it, and then walked out and climbed up into her flower throne.

Just then the sun was high in the heavens, and all the fairies came trooping up to be numbered.

The Queen was very happy to see so many of her subjects all at once, and she nodded and smiled at each one as she gave the number – 'One, two, three, four, five, six,' and so on. About the time she got to 'seventy-seven, seventy-eight, seventy-nine,' she got pretty hoarse, but she was a determined little queen, and very anxious to number all her subjects in one day, so she kept bravely on – 'one twenty-nine, one thirty, one thirty-one,' and so forth.

When she reached 'one sixty-seven, one sixty-eight, one sixty-nine,' she was so sleepy she could hardly keep her eyes open, and she had forgotten all about her lace dress and golden crown and pearl slippers. All she could think about was keeping her eyes open and saying the numbers straight.

'Three forty-seven,' – her voice grew softer – 'three – forty – eight, three – forty – ni...' Her voice trailed off to nothing; the Fairy Queen was fast asleep.

Now of course when a queen goes to sleep everybody has to wait quietly until she wakes up, unless the queen has ordered them to call her. So all the fairy people sat down where they were and whispered quietly together and waited. But she slept quite a little while – until the sun began to drop in the sky and everybody was wondering how in the world she was to get through all the rest of the numbering that day – when she awoke.

She sat right up on her throne, and looking around, said, 'Why are you all sitting about there, looking at *me?*'

Everybody was a little frightened, for they didn't wish to displease her. Finally a little girl fairy right under the throne plucked up courage to say, 'If you please, O Queen, you told us to come and be numbered, and so we're waiting for you to begin again.'

Then the Queen remembered all about it – that she had sent for them to be numbered and that she had numbered as far as three forty-nine and gone to sleep. She looked around at the hosts of fairies yet to be numbered, and she looked at the sun fast sinking in the sky, and exclaimed, 'I think numbering fairies is a *very* stupid business!'

All the fairies nodded their heads and waited, for they had no idea what she would do next.

'I don't want you numbered, anyway. Think how it would sound to say, 'Nine Hundred and Sixty-seven, come carry my train!'

Then she noticed for the first time that every fairy was dressed in his or her very best clothes in honour of the day, and that every single fairy had stuck in the front of their hair a favourite flower or leaf or twig.

A happy thought occurred to her. She waved her magic wand over the host of fairies and cried, 'All the flowers and twigs and leaves that you wear in your hair shall stay fresh forever, and your name shall be the name of that which is on your brow!'

And to this day every fairy wears something – a spotted leaf, a green twig, a white violet, or a yellow stem – in the front of his hair, and when you wish to call a fairy by name you look at his forehead and call him Spotted Leaf, or Green Twig, or whatever you see on his brow.

And so the fairies were named.

JUST A BEGINNING

O NCE upon a time, in the long, long ago, this world was just a baby world and everything on it was very different from the way it is now – oh, very different!

All the flowers, in all the forests, were snow-white in that long-ago time when the world was a baby world, for babies always have white things around them. So all the flowers were white, and the clouds were white, and the soft, white snow covered the ground all winter through, so the dead, brown leaves could hide.

In those days the world seemed very small and baby-ish instead of big and covered with oceans and mountains and cities. Of course, it wasn't really truly little, for worlds don't grow bigger as people do – but the things on them change, something like the lines on people's faces.

But you see, in that long-ago time there were no aeroplanes in which people could fly up and see how big the world really was; and there were no trains to take people a long distance; and there were no boats to carry people across the ocean. The only way to get anywhere was to walk, and you know when you just walk you can't go very far or find out very much about the world. Try it some day. Walk as far as you can – then shut your eyes and pretend you know only what you have seen on that walk! You don't know much about Italy or China that way, do you?

It wouldn't have done any good if there had been aeorplanes and trains and boats, for there were no people to ride in them. Nobody lived on earth then – only fairies, and fairies don't ride on trains. And really, the fairies then cared very little for exploring the world and finding out how big it was and such things, for each band of fairies was so happy in its own forest and playing by its own brook that there was no time to look in other forests.

Each little fairy slept in a flower at night.

You see, the world was different then in a good many ways. For one thing, the fairies hadn't learned the difference between work and play. So, bright and early, they got up and did all the things they had to do. Then they did all the things they wanted to do; and they couldn't tell which was the most fun. Wasn't that a joke on the fairies?

Each little fairy slept in a flower at night, so just before sunrise the flower would unfold its petals ever so little, to wake the fairy up. Then the fairy would open his eyes and stretch – oh, it's such fun to stretch good and hard in the morning – and that would make the flower open out wide so the fairy could jump down to the ground.

Of course all the brothers and sisters and cousins of fairies got up in just the same way and at the same time, and they all had a very jolly scramble down to the brook to take their baths. They thought it was lots of fun to take a bath in the brook.

After they had splashed around awhile and got all freshened up, they each dipped the tips of their fingers in the water and ran as fast as they could back to the flower where they had slept.

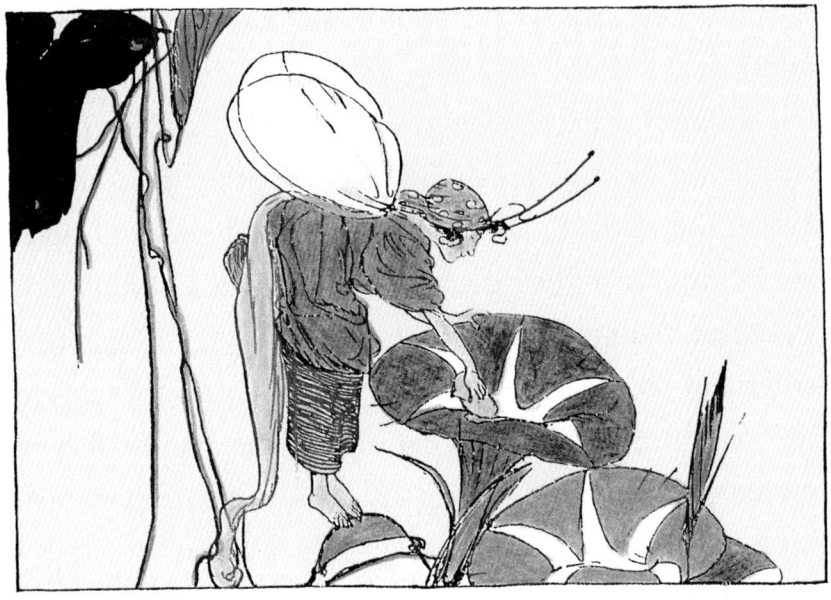

Fairies wash the flowers every day, even now.

There they shook their fingers over the flower so that the glittering drops washed the petals. Fairies wash the flowers every day, even now – only grown folks don't know it. They sleep until after the fairies are in hiding for the day (nowadays fairies play only at night; that's the reason you never see them), and then when people get up and walk into their gardens, and see the fresh drops of water on the flowers, they say,

14

'Oh, see the dew!' And they never even think about the fairies.

By that time the fairies were so hungry they couldn't think of anything but breakfast. So they folded their arms, stood on tiptoe and fluttered their wings, and up they flew to the nearest flower for breakfast. All night long the flowers had been working so that in the morning a golden drop of honey lay in the heart of each blossom, all ready for some little fairy to come and eat it. That's an easy way to get breakfast, I'm sure!

After that, all the little fairies went to school and the big fairies tended to their work so they could surely be through by afternoon and all play together before sundown. At the close of day, when the sun had gone to rest for the night and the stars had lit their candles so the fairies could see to go to bed, each fairy snuggled down into his own little flower bed and dreamed of the wonderful things he would do the next day.

And that was a day in the long ago.

SUNSHINE FLOWERS

WHITE Violet was a dainty little fairy maid with golden hair and filmy wings. Her dresses were always of the finest of white satin and she wore a tiny gold chain around her hair, and a pure white violet hung from the chain right above her brow. She played and romped and had a beautiful time all day, and never bothered about her clothes at all, for if they showed the least sign of getting mussed and soiled she would stop her work or play and say, 'Muscus, cleanus!' Quick as a flash they would all be clean again, and pressed as nice as you please! That's an easy way to get freshly dressed, isn't it?

One morning White Violet finished all the work she had to do and started off with Green Twig and Silver Grass to play in the forest. Their favourite place was where a tiny spring bubbled out of the side of the hill and ran trickling down over the white pebbles to join the brook in the valley. When the bright drops dripped from pebble to pebble, they made gorgeous rainbows on which the fairies played jump-the-rope. Then, when they tired of that, they played London Bridge on rainbows.

One side would stand on one bow and the leader would reach across to the leader on the next rainbow, and then the side that broke down would tumble helter-skelter into the water. Then such shouting and splashing as there was! And when they all stood laughing and dripping on the dry bank, they shook themselves and shouted, 'Muscus, cleanus!' and in a twinkle everybody was as clean and tidy and fresh as could be, and off they scampered for more fun!

'Let's play giant in the cave,' said Green Twig, for all boys, even fairy boys, love to play pirates and giants, and such games. They went around to the other side of the hill where there was a beautiful mossy cave, and spent the rest of the morning playing giant.

About noon, White Violet was lying at one side of the cave where the great giant (Green Twig) had thrown her, when she looked toward the door and noticed ever so many sunbeams dancing in the air.

'Oh,' she cried, jumping to her feet, 'let's not play giant any more – let's catch sunbeams, and after we have a great, great many, we'll play a game with them!'

Green Twig thought that wouldn't be much fun, for he couldn't see any sunbeams, and anyway he liked to be the giant. But Silver Grass was charmed with the idea. White Violet showed Green Twig some tiny sunbeams dancing in the air, and he at once became interested and agreed to catch as many as he could for the game.

'But how shall we carry the sunbeams after we have caught them?' asked Silver Grass.

'Oh, just in your hands, I guess,' said White Violet, who really hadn't thought anything about it except that it would be fun to catch them.

'That won't do for me!' shouted Green Twig. 'I have a handful already!' And sure enough, while the others were barely getting started, he had caught a whole handful of dancing sunbeams, and was vainly trying to stuff them into his pocket.

"Will you spin us a bag to put our sunbeams in?"

'I know a better scheme than that,' said White Violet merrily. 'We can find some spiders and have them weave bags for our sunbeams.'

'Just the thing!' shouted Green Twig and Silver Grass together. And off the three scampered to where three fat green and black spiders were busily spinning silvery nets from branch to branch on the bushes.

'If you please,' said White Violet to the fattest and jolliest of the three, 'will you spin us a bag to put our sunbeams in?'

'Of course, we'll be glad to,' said the spider, and he and his brothers went to work. In a twinkle three dainty bags were ready, and White Violet and Green Twig and Silver Grass thanked the spiders, slung the bags on their shoulders, and started off to catch the sunbeams.

All afternoon they ran and flew over the meadows and through the woods, catching the golden beams and putting them in their cobweb bags.

Other fairies, seeing them having such a jolly time, called out, 'What are you doing? What are you putting in your bags?' And the three fairies would reply, 'We're catching sunbeams! Don't you want to get some?' The other fairies always said they did, so before long *all* the fairies were chasing sunbeams.

Nobody noticed that the big old sun was getting lower and lower, and that the birds were going to their nests, until – all of a sudden, it seemed – the sun was gone and there were no more sunbeams to catch! Then everybody sat down and drew a long breath and wondered what in the world they would do with the sunbeams now they had them.

'I'll tell you what we can do,' said White Violet. 'We're all too tired to play with our sunbeams tonight, so let's put them in our flower beds and go to sleep, and then in the morning we'll be ready to play with them the very first thing.'

Everybody thought that was a fine idea. So all the fairies who had started late and gathered only a few sunbeams sprinkled them in the centre of the flower, then climbed in, pulled the petals shut, and went to sleep.

Those who had started early and had a bag full of sunbeams, dumped their bright gold in the centre of the flower and all over the sides too.

And every fairy went to sleep – and they slept so soundly they never knew that in the middle of the night the Fairy Queen waved her wand in a dream, and changed all the sunbeams to gold and melted the gold into the flower. The fairies never even guessed when she did it!

But in the morning when they woke up, there, in the very centre of every flower, was a spot of gold, and the flowers that were entirely full of sunbeams the night before were all turned to gold.

And ever since then there have been some golden flowers – buttercups, golden glows, and marigolds – but in the heart of every flower is a spot of gold where the sunbeams lay.

Ever since then there have been some golden flowers.

PANSIES FOR THOUGHTS

ONE morning the Fairy Queen wakened with a feeling that she was going to think of something *very* nice, but she couldn't quite tell what it was. All the time she was taking her bath and watering her flower bed and tidying her palace she tried to remember what the *very* nice thing was, but she couldn't remember. Then, just as she was going to climb into her flower throne, she suddenly knew – 'Why, of course!' she exclaimed. 'I am going to have a party! I dreamed all about it!'

So she climbed up into her flower throne and called her messengers to her.

'Go quickly,' she commanded, 'and tell all the fairies in my kingdom that I will have a party this afternoon, and they must come to it.'

So the messengers flew quickly over the kingdom and told all the fairies they were invited to the Queen's party that very afternoon.

Then indeed there was hurrying and scurrying in the forest, for the Queen's parties were rare treats and every single fairy wished to look their very best. The spiders were busy weaving lace frocks, and along the sides of the brook were rows of fairies combing their hair and arranging their jewellery while they looked in the water mirror.

About noon everybody was ready to go when Leaf Bud said to Smooth Pebble, 'Don't you think we ought to take the Queen a present? Maybe it's her birthday.'

'Yes,' said Smooth Pebble thoughtfully, 'I think that's a very nice idea; but what shall we take? The Queen already has everything she wants.'

'I know,' said little Leaf Bud. 'We can take her a fresh flower – nobody has enough of those!'

'Just the thing!' replied Smooth Pebble brightly. 'Let's tell everybody we see to take her a pansy!'

So they did. Everybody was so glad to take a present to the Queen that when all had laid their flowers before her the ground was nearly covered

All the fairies wished to look their very best.

with snow-white pansies – there were no coloured ones then, you know.

The Queen was very happy to think her subjects had been so thoughtful as to bring her lovely gifts. She was anxious to keep the flowers fresh and new, so she asked all the fairies to stand their pansies in the brook – at the edge – until the party was over, and they did. The brook looked very strange and very pretty with its border of white pansies along each bank.

After the flowers were fixed the fairies played many kinds of games for an hour. By that time they were tired enough to sit down on the smooth grass and eat the dinner the Queen had prepared for them. There was honey and dew in tiny cups, and every good thing that fairies enjoy.

But they couldn't understand what the odd, silvery pile of threads in the centre of the circle was for. When all had finished eating, the Queen said, 'This centre pile is a pile of cobweb threads – the beginnings are here and the ends are somewhere in the forest. Go and search for the end, for there you will find a gift from me.'

With merry shouts each fairy picked up a cobweb and started off to find his gift. They had to go very carefully, for cobwebs are easily broken, and these crossed and re-crossed each other many times.

White Violet and Leaf Bud found theirs ran close together, so they helped each other over hard places and at the end found their gifts on either side of a smooth, flat rock. And what do you suppose the gifts were? Magic paint boxes!

White Violet knew at once what hers was for, and started to paint some pictures on the rock. She painted clouds and trees and birds, and was so happy that she forgot all about being polite, until Leaf Bud reminded her. Together they picked up their boxes and started back to thank the Queen.

There they found dozens of happy fairies, laughing and shouting and thanking the Queen for their gifts.

'Dear friends,' said the Queen, holding up her hands for them to keep quiet, 'I am so glad you like the paint boxes. Now I'll tell you how to use them; they are magic paints, and anything you paint with them will stay coloured that way forever, so be very careful how you use them. Now, for a beginning, I want each of you to paint for me the white pansy you brought me today!'

'How shall we paint it?' asked Leaf Bud. 'What colours do you like best?'

'I like all the colours,' answered the Queen. 'You must look at what you like best, and paint the colour that it makes you think about.'

So the fairies all set to work, and everything was very quiet except for the swish of their brushes and the sounds of mixing paint.

White Violet looked up at the clear blue sky, and painted her pansy dainty blue with flecks of white. Leaf Bud looked at the golden sun, and painted hers yellow, with streaks of black for the branches of the trees she saw against the sky. Green Twig thought of the dark corners of the forest, and painted deep purple like the dusky shadows. Spotted Leaf thought of the twilight, and painted the rose of the clouds, the blue of the sky, and the purple of the coming night all on the face of one flower.

But poor little Silver Moss thought and thought so hard about what colour he should paint his flower, that he fell off the rock he was sitting on and

Silver Moss tumbled into the brook and spilled all his paint.

tumbled into the brook and spilled *all* his paint. So one little pansy stayed pure white.

When the flowers were finished the queen was delighted with them. 'I think these are much prettier than all white ones,' she said gravely, 'for when I look at *these* pansies I can guess what you were thinking about.'

So she waved her wand and ordered that all pansies ever after should be coloured like those.

And the party was over.

So always the pansies are coloured for the skies and the trees and the shadows and the sunshine, and every pansy stands for a loving thought.

Published Oct. 1998 by Windjammer Publishing,
White Clouds, Perranporth, Cornwall TR6 0DZ, U.K.

This Edition © Windjammer Publishing.

ISBN No. 1 900234 06 8

'Forest Fairies' was originally published in 1915,
by Rand McNally (Chicago, U.S.A.), under the title
'Flower Fairies.'

WINDJAMMER PUBLISHING